HAMISH HAMILTON LTD

Published by the Penguin Group
27 Wrights Lane, London W8 5TZ, England
Viking Penguin Inc, 375 Hudson Street, New York, New York 10014, U.S.A.
Penguin Books Australia Ltd, Ringwood, Victoria, Australia.
Penguin Books Canada Ltd, 10 Alcorn Avenue, Toronto, Ontario, Canada M4V3B2
Penguin Books (NZ) Ltd, 182-190 Wairau Road Auckland 10, New Zealand.

Penguin Books Ltd, Registered Offices: Harmondsworth, Middlesex, England.

First Published in Great Britain 1991
by Hamish Hamilton Ltd

Copyright © 1991 by Babette Cole

1 3 5 7 9 10 8 6 4 2

British Library Cataloguing in Publication Data
CIP data for this book is available from the British Library

ISBN 0-241-13133-2

Originated by Brian Gregory Associates Ltd, St Albans, U.K.
Printed and bound by L.E.G.O, Vicenza, Italy.

Tarzanna lived in the jungle

with the animals.

One day she saw a
new kind of animal
she hadn't seen before

so she carried it off!

The new animal was
a boy called
Gerald.

He was studying
spiders.

Tarzanna taught him to speak animalese.
He taught her English.
"Why don't you visit my country?" said Gerald.
"O.K." said Tarzanna.

The animals did not want Tarzanna to go.

But she wanted to ride
in the helicopter.

Tarzanna didn't like Gerald's country!

Gerald's mum and dad were nice. They knew
she missed the animals so they promised
to take her to the zoo.

This was a serious mistake…

because she and Gerald could
speak animalese.
"Let us out, Tarzanna!"
said the animals.

So later, when it got dark

that's exactly what Tarzanna and Gerald did!

They took them back
to the flat...

but Gerald's mum just couldn't stand his spiders!

Tarzanna, Gerald and the animals ran away.

They hid out in the poshest boxes they could find. But the snooty shoppers were scared stiff!

There were
pickpockets
about…

...but they didn't like what was in Gerald's pocket!

"This is an awful way to live," complained Gerald. "The animals will start eating people if they don't get some dinner soon."

"We'll go and ask the Prime Minister," said Tarzanna. "He'll know what to do."

But the Prime Minister was
a bit tied up at the time!

SECRET PAPERS

Toffee Papers

Tarzanna, Gerald and the animals rescued the Prime Minister!

SECRET PAPERS

"Lucky the animals were so hungry,"
Tarzanna said.

When the fuss was over, Gerald's parents
came for Tarzanna and Gerald...

...and the zoo man
came for the animals!

"Wait!" commanded the Prime Minister
in a muffled voice.
"Everyone can go back
to the jungle!"

He bought them all first-class tickets home on Jungle Airways

The jungle animals loved
the zoo animals and
Gerald's dad built
a smashing
tree house.

"Doesn't your mum
mind the spiders?"
asked Tarzanna.

"I told her there wouldn't be any *spiders*
in the bath in the jungle! said Gerald.